For the children of Mile 18

©1971, Ann Blades

Published simultaneously in Canada by
Tundra Books of Montreal, Quebec H3G 1J6

and in the United States by
Tundra Books of Northern New York, Plattsburgh, N.Y. 12901

Printing History

1971	1st Printing
1972	"Book of the Year" award of
	Canadian Association of Children's Librarians
1973	2nd Printing
1975	1st Paperback Printing
	2nd Paperback Printing (school edition)
1976	3rd Paperback Printing
	1st Library Edition
	U.K. and Commonwealth edition, Bodley Head, London, England
	German Language edition, Jungbrunnen Verlag, Vienna, Austria

Canadian ISBN   (Paperback) 0-88776-059-7
         ISBN   (Library edition) 0-88776-025-2

U.S.   ISBN   (Paperback) 0-912766-34-4
         ISBN   (Library edition) 0-912766-44-1

Printed in Canada, Library Edition bound in the United States

Mary of Mile 18

Story and pictures by Ann Blades

Tundra Books
Montreal
Canada

Tundra Books
Plattsburgh, N.Y.
U.S.A.

It is a cold winter in northern
British Columbia. At the Fehr farm
snow has covered the ground
since early November and it will
not melt until May.

One clear night in February the
temperature drops to forty degrees
below zero and the northern lights
flash across the sky. Mary Fehr
gets out of bed and goes to the
window to watch and listen. She
hears a crackling sound and smiles,
excited. Mary likes to pretend
that if she hears the music of the
lights, the next day will bring
something special.

The next morning Mary Fehr wakes up happy. At first she can't think why. Then she remembers, and wonders what the day will bring. She pulls on her boots, hat, heavy coat and mitts, and walks to the henhouse to feed the chickens.

One winter day is so much like the next. What could happen? Her mother is expecting a new baby, but it is not supposed to arrive for another month.

Mary feeds the chickens and starts
back. Seeing the house in front
of her reminds her of another special
day, the day her father finished
building it. He was so proud. When
the family first moved to the farm,
they lived in the shack where the
grain is now kept. Before that they
lived in town, but Mary does not
remember so far back.

Mary's mother has told her of the
comforts of town: water taps,
electricity, telephones and television.
Here, water is brought into the
house a pail at a time; the sink drains
into another pail which is carried
outside and emptied. The bathroom is
an outhouse and the bathtub is a
big bucket. The family has a transistor
radio to listen to, but Mrs. Fehr gets
lonely sometimes.

The closest neighbors are the Bergens,
and their farm is two miles away.

Mary sees her father near the barn.
The caterpillar was damaged
yesterday, and he is trying to fix it.
Every winter day when it does not
snow, Mr. Fehr likes to clear a little
more land. He uses the cat to
push the trees down and into piles.

When summer comes all the family
will pick roots, tearing them out
of the earth with their hands so that
the land can be planted.

"When we clear most of this land,
the Government will give us the
deed to it," her father explained.
"This is why we have moved north;
so that we can have our own farm
and live our own way."

Before he comes in for breakfast,
Mr. Fehr puts a propane torch
under the truck to warm the engine.
It will take an hour to warm
because last night was so cold.

Usually Mary likes this time just
before they set out for school.
Mr. Fehr is playing with little Eva.
Isaac and Jake are looking at
a book from the class library. This
morning Sarah tries to get Mary
to crayon with her, but Mary can't
keep her mind on it. What could
happen today? She is anxious to get
to school.

Mrs. Fehr serves breakfast. After the
new baby comes, the girls will
help even more than now. They will
do dishes, cook meals, make beds
and scrub floors. But they won't mind.
A new baby is so exciting.

The radio is on. The weather report is:
"Snow this afternoon. Clearing and
colder towards evening."

Mr. Fehr goes out first and starts
the engine. He lets it run for a
while, then honks the horn. Mary,
Sarah, Jake and Isaac come out and
crowd into the seat beside him.
It is a tight squeeze, but it is also nice
and warm.

Today the teacher, Mrs. Burns,
has turned the oil heater on full, but
the room is still so cold that the
children sitting beside the windows
keep their coats on and edge closer
to the heater. At noontime Sarah
watches the class while Mrs. Burns
goes to the back to have her lunch.
At three o'clock Mary helps dress the
smaller children. She ties their
scarves over their heads and across
their faces to protect them from
the cold.

Mary sighs as she pulls on her own
overshoes. School is over for the day
and still nothing special has happened.

In the truck on the way home,
Mr. Fehr listens to the children talk
about school but does not talk
himself. He is watching the road
carefully. Snow is drifting and it
is hard to see.

Just as they near their farm, another
truck looms out of the blowing
snow. Mr. Fehr steers quickly to the
right to avoid an accident and
his back wheels slide into the ditch.

As Mary watches her father jack up
the truck and put chains on the rear
tires, she thinks, ''I hope *that's*
not the special thing.''

Then, farther up the road to the
house, Mary sees something in the
snow and cries: ''Look, a puppy.''
She runs to him, kneels down, and
the puppy licks her mitt.

Mary carries the pup to the truck.
"Please, father, can I keep him?"

Mr. Fehr shakes his head. "You
know the rules. Our animals must
work for us or give us food."

Mary protests: "A dog can help . . . ."

Mr. Fehr interrupts: "That isn't a
regular dog. He's part wolf,
and wolf-pups are useless. Take him
into the woods and leave him.
Come on the rest of you. Chores."

Sadly Mary goes off with the pup
while the others go about their jobs.
Jake goes to the woodpile, takes
an axe, splits logs and carries them,
an armful at a time, into the
house. Both the wood stove that
Mrs. Fehr uses for cooking and
the barrel heater that warms the house
take a lot of wood. Sometimes even
when both are going, the house is
chilly.

The pup snuggles in Mary's arms
as she carries him into the woods.
How she wishes she could keep him!
''I would call you Wolf,'' she says.

It has stopped snowing, but the
path is covered over and the trees
seem to grow closer and closer
together. If she goes too far from
the road, she might not be able
to find her way back. She puts the
pup down to see what will happen.
He runs around, excited, sniffing
at the trees. She turns and walks
away. He does not follow.

''That was something special
alright,'' Mary thinks, as she walks
home, ''but it didn't last for long.''

Near the house Isaac passes her
on their horse, Mouse. A few years
ago Isaac and Jake rode Mouse
to school and kept her in the barn
behind the schoolhouse. But now
Mouse has to wait until Isaac gets
home to go for a run.

The house smells of fresh-baked
bread as Mary enters. Her mother
looks up from the stove.

"Where have you been, Mary?
Sarah is waiting for you. I'm almost
out of water."

Silently Mary bends down, takes
two empty buckets standing near the
door and goes out.

Sarah has already filled her
buckets with snow. Mary does the
same and the two girls carry the
snow into the house and dump it
into a big barrel. They wait for
it to melt, then go out for more snow.

From the barrel comes all the water
for drinking, cooking and washing.
Tomorrow Mrs. Fehr will wash clothes
and Sarah will stay home to help,
so the barrel must be full tonight. In
spring and summer, it is much
easier. A barrel catches rain water
from the roof, and the river is
unfrozen. But in winter all the water
comes from snow. When the snow
is dry and powdery like today, it takes
many trips to fill the barrel.

Each time Mary goes out, she looks
toward the woods. Her father comes
out of the barn where he has been
feeding the pigs and goes into the
house. Isaac returns with Mouse. The
pup is nowhere in sight.

The coal oil lamp is lit and Mary
sits at the table staring at her
reader. Mrs. Fehr is making supper.
Mr. Fehr is cleaning his gun. The
radio says another cold night, and
Mary thinks about the pup.

Suddenly there is a sound outside
the door, a low whimper. Mr. Fehr
goes to the door and opens it. Mary
cries: ''It's little Wolf,'' and
rushes to take the pup in her arms.

Mr. Fehr is angry. ''Why are you
encouraging him to stay around? Get
your coat on and get rid of him so
that he doesn't come back.''

This time Mary walks nearly two
miles to the Bergen farm. ''Perhaps
Mr. Bergen will let his children
keep you,'' she says, putting Wolf
down near the door. ''Then I can see
you sometimes.''

As she runs home in the cold night
her toes and fingertips sting and the
air burns her throat.

The family is at the supper table
when she gets back. Her mother looks
up, says: "We have your favorite
supper tonight, Mary. Moose steak."

"I don't want to eat, mother."

Mrs. Fehr starts to object; but
Mr. Fehr stops her: "Let the girl go to
bed without eating if she wants to."
His voice is still angry. "She should
not have asked to keep the animal.
She knows the rules."

Mary gets into bed and buries her
head in her pillow. "Why should he
be so angry?" she wonders. Then
she remembers last fall when Jake
and Isaac begged their father
for a gun of their own. He refused
and got angry then, too. Her mother
explained: "Your father gives you
everything he can. When you ask for
more, it hurts him to refuse. That
is why he gets angry."

Mary lies thinking about this until
she falls asleep.

That night when everyone in the
Fehr house is asleep, another
kind of animal, a coyote, comes out
of the woods. He sniffs at all
the buildings, then stops at the
henhouse. Silently he paws at
the rope that holds the door shut,
and the rope comes loose. The
coyote pushes the door to enter the
henhouse and get at the chickens.

Suddenly, a shrill screech goes up
in the night.

Everyone in the Fehr house wakes up.
Mr. Fehr throws his clothes on
quickly, grabs his gun and goes out.

The rest of the family get up and
crowd around the window to see
what is happening. All except Mary.
She hears Isaac say, ''It's just
a coyote,'' and she tries to go back
to sleep, so that she won't have
to think about little Wolf out in
the woods.

Mr. Fehr sees the coyote in the
bright light from the snow. He aims
his gun and fires.

His first shot misses. The coyote
turns, snarling, then quickly runs
behind the henhouse. Mr. Fehr fires
again, but the coyote takes off and
disappears over the hill.

Mr. Fehr goes to the henhouse,
looks inside to make sure the chickens
are alright. Then he carefully ties
the door tight. He is about to return to
the house when he sees something
at his feet.

It is the wolf-pup wagging his tail.

"So it was you who warned us,"
Mr. Fehr says. He bends down,
takes the puppy in his hands and
looks at him. "Tough little fellow,
aren't you? Not afraid of cold or
coyotes. Maybe you will earn your
keep after all."

He carries the pup into the house.
Mrs. Fehr has lit the oil lamp and
everyone is waiting for him, except
Mary.

The children get excited when they
see the wolf-pup. Mr. Fehr puts
his finger to his lips as a sign for
them to be silent. He goes to the
bedroom.

33

Mary looks up as her father comes
into the bedroom. He puts the
wolf-pup down on the bed. "This
little fellow would like to get
warm," he says.

Mary can hardly believe she is
not dreaming as she takes little Wolf
in her arms. "Can I keep him?"
she asks.

"I suppose you can," her father
answers gruffly.

In the doorway of the bedroom,
Isaac and Jake and Sarah and
Mrs. Fehr, holding Eva in her arms,
are all standing watching and
smiling.

Mile 18 is a real place, even though it
is too small to appear on the map
of Canada. If you would like to visit it,
you must travel north on the Alaska
Highway for seventy-three miles, then
turn right onto a gravel road. When
you have driven eighteen miles along
this road, you will come to the little
Mennonite community of Mile 18
where the Fehrs and the Bergens live.
If you would like some idea of where
it is on the map, the closest town
is Fort St. John, British Columbia,
forty-five miles away.

Ann Blades and her husband taught
school at Mile 18 a few years ago.
She came to love its children so much
that she wrote and painted this story
for them.